Off to the beach!

© Disney

Mickey is ready for sun.

Sunscreen is a must.

© Disney

How many beach balls do you count?

Your Answer:

Minnie dances the hula.

Catch!

What a sand castle!

Match each character
to the correct signature.

Mickey Mouse

Minnie Mouse

PLUTO

daisy duck

Dot-to-dot

Minnie hears the ocean.

Which character's line leads to Minnie?

A

B

C

Your Answer:

Answer: B

Beach Volleyball

Speedboat Mickey helps
Minnie learn to ski.

"Let's have a picnic on the beach."

"My cheese!"

Ready to dive!

Minnie catches a dolphin wave!

Pluto

Draw Pluto.

Wow! Treasure!

What a sweet fishy.

A huge pearl!

Help Donald and Daisy find Mickey and Minnie.

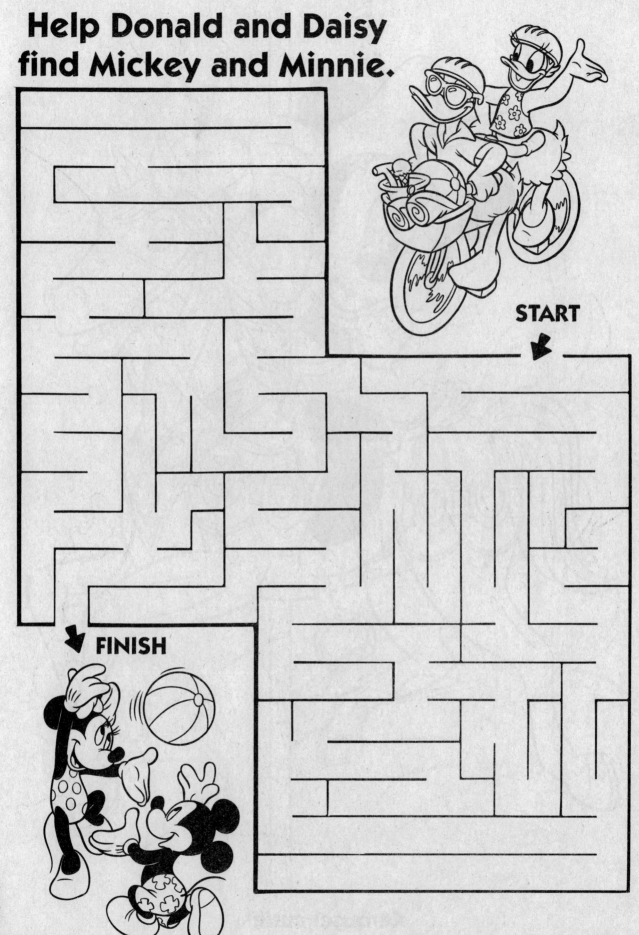

START

FINISH

Carousel cutie!

Dot-to-dot

"Aw, shucks..."

"Gosh!"

Draw your favorite Disney character.

Skyride buddies!

Fun with Friends

Time for Fun

How many words can you make from the letters in:

MINNIE AND FRIENDS

_____

_____

_____

_____

_____

_____

"Hello, little friend!"

"Tee-hee!"

Write a song for Goofy to sing.

Hooray!

This is your day!

Which one doesn't belong?

A

B

C

Your Answer:

Answer: B

Mickey performs magic.

All set for supper.

© Disney

Goofy samples the cookies.

Daisy has a green thumb.

Minnie has a pretty garden.

"Say cheese!"

"Say cheese!"

"Yum! Cheese!"

Game time!

Which piece completes the picture?

A   B   C   D

Your Answer:

Tackled!

Oof!

Minnie Mouse

Draw Minnie Mouse.

Mickey tries his backhand.

"Hit it, Minnie!"

© Disney

Ready to take the field.

Minnie dribbles the soccer ball.

© Disney

G-O-O-O-O-O-A-L!

Find the 5 differences in the picture below.

Mickey aims his polo mallet.

Minnie is an elegant equestrian.

Mickey flops over the high-jump bar.

Minnie is graceful on inline skates.

Mickey takes up archery.

Oops!

All for one, and one for all!